Free Association

Where my mind goes during science class

Written by
Barbara Esham

Illustrated by
Mike Gordon

Digital color by
MOLLY HAHN

Editor
LINA RAYE DAYTON

Click, click, click, click... Oh, right! I'm in SCIENCE class!
The sound of Mrs. Freedman's shoes startled me back to class again.

Have you ever started to think about one thing and ended up thinking about something completely different? I do it all the time.

We're learning about the Arctic Circle in science. I was following along, but then I suddenly became distracted by one of my adventurous ideas.

I started thinking about my boogie board and how much
fun it might be if I took it to the Arctic Circle.

"Emily, please pay attention. The test is next Monday, and I'm concerned you will not be prepared," Mrs. Freedman whispered as she turned four pages of my textbook.

I love science. Really, I do, but I can tell Mrs. Freedman doesn't think so.
She has this extraordinary ability to catch me right in the middle of what
I'm NOT supposed to be thinking about. I guess my daydream adventures
keep me from following along in class.

I have always loved exploring new ideas and doing experiments. I thought science was going to be my favorite class. It seems like the only thing we do in science is memorize information from our book. Science class just doesn't seem like science to me. Is this what Albert Einstein did?

"Emily, I need you to pay attention. You are two pages behind the class again," Mrs. Freedman said in her frustrated voice.

"I'm sorry, Mrs. Freedman. I was thinking about Albert Einstein," I replied with a whisper.

"Well, Emily, I'm sure Albert Einstein would suggest that you follow along with the class," Mrs. Freedman added. The rest of the class giggled. I felt like crawling under my desk.

To make matters worse, Mrs. Freedman announced, "Emily Taylor, I would like to see you before lunch today."

I wish that I could just dig a hole to the other side of the world to escape this embarrassment.

My entire class went to lunch, but I stayed behind to talk with Mrs. Freedman. She got right down to business. "You are a smart girl, Emily, but I am concerned about the difficulty you are having with focusing in class," she said in a serious voice.

"I thought of an exercise that might help keep you on track in class.
The next time you daydream or become distracted during class,
I would like for you to write about it in this journal," she said.

"Even if I'm thinking about riding a giant wave on my boogie board?"

14

"Yes, even if you are thinking about your boogie board," said Mrs. Freedman.

"The purpose of the exercise is to help you notice when you are distracted. I have a feeling this will help you recognize what is important, and what is NOT important to think about during science class," she added.

The next day in science class, I opened my new journal, just in case I became distracted. As we were learning more about the Arctic Circle, I started thinking about some great ideas that weren't exactly about what we were learning. Mrs. Freedman might consider my ideas distractions, so I began to write them down in my journal, just in case.

Mrs. Freedman suddenly appeared behind me and whispered,
"Emily, I would like to see you after class."

Oh no, I guess I'm in trouble again.

"Emily, you spent half the class writing!"
Mrs. Freedman exclaimed with a frown.

18

"Mrs. Freedman, I wrote all of my ideas in my journal. Some of my ideas are about science and the Arctic Circle, but not exactly what we were working on in class," I replied nervously.

"For a minute, I did daydream about my friend's sleepover this weekend and how we plan to polish her brother's nails while he is sleeping," I explained, blushing of course.

"I would like to read your journal to have a better understanding of what is distracting you in class," said Mrs. Freedman, as she gently took the journal from my hands.

Oh no! I wish that I hadn't mentioned the sleepover at all!
I only thought about it for a few seconds, and I stopped
daydreaming about it once I wrote in the journal.
How will I ever become a scientist if I can't make it through
fourth grade science?

The next day Mrs. Freedman seemed very happy.

She was holding my journal and smiling.

22

"Class, one of your classmates has created a theory to explore the differences between penguins and flight birds. She has also made a list of changes she believes penguins would need in order to survive in a warmer environment."

"From now on, each of you can create a science journal to let your inventive imaginations soar! This is what science is all about — creating new ideas and using your imaginations," Mrs. Freedman said with a smile.

During lunch, Mrs. Freedman came up to me and said, "Emily, your creative thinking skills are quite advanced for a student your age."

"Thank you, Mrs. Freedman... but what creative thinking skills are we talking about?" I asked with a nervous laugh.

"Your penguin theory, of course. Remember this, Emily Taylor: theories, creative thought, and persistence, along with a bit of tolerance for the required work, will lead you to success."

"Oh! THOSE creative thinking skills! I was afraid you were going to mention my theory on the best way to polish Claire's brother's fingernails."

Mrs. Freedman giggled, "I am sure your theory will help you discover the best way to complete that experiment."

The end.

Free Association, Where My Mind Goes During Science Class
Endorsements and Reviews

"As an affective neuroscientist and an educational psychologist, I can tell you that two things are especially important for children's school learning: feeling emotionally validated and having a good awareness of one's own learning. These books offer a rare combination for young students—they teach both of these things!" ~Mary Helen Immordino-Yang

Mary Helen Immordino-Yang is a neuroscientist and human development psychologist who studies the neural, psychophysiological and psychological bases of social emotion, self-awareness and culture and their implications for development and schools. She is an Assistant Professor of Education at the Rossier School of Education, an Assistant Professor of Psychology at the Brain and Creativity Institute, and a member of the Neuroscience Graduate Program Faculty at the University of Southern California.

"Today's children are taught to pay attention at all times, follow rules unquestioningly, and do well on one-size-fits-all tests. Mountains of psychological research clearly show how none of this is conducive to creativity and innovation. In The Adventures of Everyday Geniuses series, Esham knows her cognitive psychology and the best ways to learn and create. She brilliantly presents entertaining, relatable stories while highlighting the importance of individual differences and the use of imagination and daydreaming. I really wish I read these books when I was younger, I know I would have felt a lot better about myself!" ~Scott Barry Kaufman Ph.D.

Scott Barry Kaufman is a cognitive psychologist specializing in the development of intelligence, creativity, and personality. He applies a variety of perspectives to come to a richer understanding and appreciation of all kinds of minds. In his latest book, Ungifted: Intelligence Redefined, he presents a new theory of human intelligence that he hopes will help all people realize their dreams. Kaufman is adjunct assistant professor of Psychology at New York University, co-founder of The Creativity Post, and author of "Beautiful Minds" at Scientific American Mind.

CATALOGING-IN-PUBLICATION DATA

Esham, Barbara.
Free association : where my mind goes during science class /
written by Barbara Esham ;   illustrated by Mike Gordon. -- 1st ed. --
Perry Hall, Md. : Mainstream Connections Publishing, 2013.
    p. ; cm.
    (The adventures of everyday geniuses)

    ISBN: 13-digit: 978-1-60336-546-8 ; 10-digit: 1-60336-546X
    Audience: Ages 5-10.
    Summary: Emily, a very creative thinker, finds it difficult to pay
attentionin science class. Her teacher, Mrs. Freedman, tries to help
Emily with her "daydreaming", only to find that Emily's creative
thinking skills are quite advanced for a student her age!--Publisher.

1. Free association (Psychology)--Juvenile fiction. 2. Gifted
children--Juvenile fiction. 3. Creative ability--Juvenile fiction.
4. Attention-deficit disordered children--Juvenile fiction.
5. Cognitive styles in children--Juvenile fiction. 6. Attention in
children--Juvenile fiction. 7. School--Juvenile fiction. 8. Self-
esteem--Juvenile fiction. 9. Child psychology--Juvenile fiction.
10. Children--Life skills guides--Juvenile fiction. 11. [Gifted
children--Fiction. 12. Creative ability--Fiction. 13. Attention-
deficit hyperactivity disorder--Fiction. 14. Attention--Fiction.
15. Learning--Fiction. 16. Schools--Fiction. 17. Self-esteem--
Fiction. 18. Behavior--Fiction. 19. Life skills--Fiction.]
20. Humorous stories. 21. Children's stories. I. Gordon, Mike,
1948 March 16- II. Title. III. Series: Esham, Barbara. Adventures
of everyday geniuses.

PZ7.E74583 F74 2013

[E]--dc23   1312

BOOK INFORMATION

Free Association, Where My Mind Goes During Science Class
Written by Barbara Esham illustrated by Mike Gordon
Published by Mainstream Connections Publishing
P.O. Box 389, Perry Hall Maryland 21128
Copyright @ 20013, Barbara Esham. All Rights Reserved
No part of this publication may be reproduced in whole or in part, in any form without
permission from the publisher. The Adventures of Everyday Geniuses is registered trademark.

Printed in Korea ~ Library Binding   Library of Congress Control Number: 2013917817

FIRST EDITION   15 14 13 12 11 10 09 08   01 02 03 04 05 06 07 08